DINOSAUR DUCKS

First published in the United States
of America in 1989 by The Mallard Press

Mallard Press and its accompanying design
and logo are trademarks of BDD Promotional
Book Company, Inc.

Produced by
Twin Books
15 Sherwood Place
Greenwich, CT 06830

ISBN 0-792-45238-0

Printed in Hong Kong

Twin Books

MALLARD PRESS

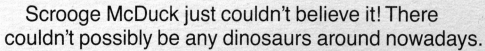

Scrooge McDuck just couldn't believe it! There couldn't possibly be any dinosaurs around nowadays.

"That's what I used to think," said Launchpad McQuack, "until I went to that island and saw them with my own eyes. I was almost squashed to death by a tyrannosaurus."

"We must leave at once!" said an excited Scrooge.

Launchpad thought it was too dangerous.

"But just think! If I could bring a diplodocus back to Duckburg, people would pay to see it!" said Scrooge.

"We'll go with you!" said his nephews.

"No," said Scrooge firmly. "You're much too young."

Huey, Dewey and Louie said the same thing to Webby when she wanted to go, too.

A few days later, supplies for the trip were put on the helicopter. One big crate held three stowaways—Scrooge's nephews. The picnic basket held another stowaway—Webby.

Soon, the helicopter was flying over a small island.
"We can still turn back," said Launchpad.
"Don't be silly!" said Scrooge. "Take us down a bit. We might see a dinosaur."
Suddenly, a dinosaur with wings flew toward them. "It's going to attack!" cried Launchpad.
The creature hit the helicopter, sending it out of control.
"Hold on!" shouted Launchpad. "We're going to crash!"

"I'll get the parachutes," said Scrooge, moving to the back of the helicopter. He found the largest box and lifted the lid. Huey, Dewey and Louie stared up at him.

"Burst me bagpipes! What are you doin' here?" cried Scrooge. "And where are the parachutes?"

"We wanted to come along, Unca Scrooge. We took all the old clothes out so that we could fit in."

As they spoke, Webby stuck her head out of the basket, but nobody noticed that she was there.

"No parachutes!" groaned Scrooge.

"Hurry, Mr. McD!" yelled Launchpad.

"Quickly, lads! Into the passenger seat and put on the safety belt," ordered Scrooge.

Launchpad fought to keep the helicopter under control.

"There are no parachutes," Scrooge told him. "You're goin' to have to land this thing."

Scrooge pulled a lever, opening a door underneath the boys' seat. As their chair dropped out of the helicopter, a parachute connected to the seat opened up. They floated to the ground safely, while a mother dinosaur and her baby looked on.

Launchpad fought bravely to land the helicopter safely.
"Hang on tight!" he cried. "We're going down!"
The helicopter crashed into a cliff, rolled over a few times,
then came to rest on a ledge.
Scrooge grabbed the picnic basket, and he and Launchpad
got out of the helicopter. Then they climbed up the cliff.

Meanwhile, the baby dinosaur was hiding behind the rocks, watching the three creatures who had fallen from the sky.

"Where's Unca Scrooge and Launchpad?" Dewey wondered. The brothers decided to try and find them. They didn't know where to begin looking, so they just picked a direction and started walking—right into the baby dinosaur!

Huey, Dewey and Louie screamed and ran. The baby dinosaur was frightened, too. He ran in the other direction.

Scrooge and Launchpad were looking for the boys.
Suddenly, they were surrounded by a group of cave-ducks.
"Stand back!" warned Scrooge. "Launchpad has a black
belt in karate!"
The cave-ducks didn't seem to understand.

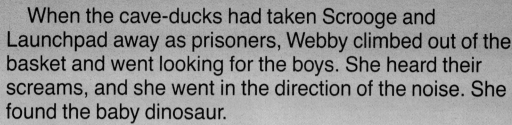

When the cave-ducks had taken Scrooge and Launchpad away as prisoners, Webby climbed out of the basket and went looking for the boys. She heard their screams, and she went in the direction of the noise. She found the baby dinosaur.

"Oh, what a cute little animal!" she cried, petting him. "Why were you afraid of him? He's so sweet!"

Scrooge's nephews were ashamed of themselves, but they were also surprised to see Webby.

"How did you get here?" asked Huey.

Webby explained that she had hidden in the picnic basket. Then she told them what had happened to Launchpad and Uncle Scrooge.

"The dinosaur can help us rescue them!" said Dewey.

"Okay," agreed his brothers. "Webby, stay here."

By this time, Launchpad and Scrooge had been tied to a tree and the leader of the cave-ducks was dancing around, wearing Scrooge's top hat!

Scrooge's nephews rode into the village on the baby dinosaur. They cut Scrooge and Launchpad loose, and tied up the leader of the cave-ducks in their place.

"Leave him there," said Scrooge, taking back his top hat, "until he learns some manners!"

23

Soon they stopped to catch their breath. "You boys were terrific!" said Scrooge. "How did you know what had happened?"

"Webby told us," said Huey, explaining how she had been hiding in the picnic basket. "But where is she? She was supposed to be waiting for us here."

They went back to the village, afraid that something had happened to Webby. They shouldn't have worried! She was sitting in front of a fire, telling a story to the cave-ducks.

Scrooge smiled. "Webby can charm the birds out of the trees, but we must go now."

The cave-duck leader grabbed Webby.

"Give her to me!" shouted Scrooge.

But the leader refused. Finally, they decided on a trade. Webby was given back to Scrooge, and Scrooge handed over his top hat!

"Let's go home!" said Scrooge, giving Webby a hug.

Suddenly, a terrible roar shook the village. The head of a giant tyrannosaurus loomed above the trees. Everyone was frightened. Then the cave-ducks led them all to the nearest cave.

But the baby dinosaur couldn't squeeze through the cave entrance!

"We've got to do something!" cried Webby.

"Don't worry," said Launchpad. "We'll get rid of that monster!"

Nearby was a stack of stone wheels, made by the cave-ducks. Launchpad took one and rolled it toward the creature. Everyone else grabbed a wheel and did the same thing. The dinosaur lost his balance, and finally fell off a cliff.

When he got back to Duckburg, Scrooge went into
business offering helicopter tours to Dinosaur Island. From
the air, people were able to see something alive from the far-
off past.

Sometimes, Webby went, too, and played with her friend,
the baby dinosaur.

JUNGLE DUCK

The plane carrying Scrooge McDuck, his nephews, Launchpad McQuack and Mrs. Beakley flew over the jungle on its way to find the legendary Silver Bird statue. As the plane prepared to land, a tear slid down Mrs. Beakley's cheek.

"Are you all right?" asked Dewey.

"It's nothing—just an old memory," she explained. "When I was nanny for Prince Greydrake, his plane disappeared over this very jungle, and he was never seen again. He would have been crowned King on his 25th birthday—the day after tomorrow."

After the plane landed, they took a small boat up the river, but only after Scrooge had bargained for the lowest price.

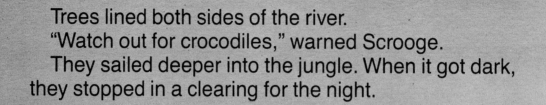

Trees lined both sides of the river.
"Watch out for crocodiles," warned Scrooge.
They sailed deeper into the jungle. When it got dark,
they stopped in a clearing for the night.

38

They ate tropical fruit for dinner.
"Delicious!" said Launchpad.
"Let's get some sleep," said Scrooge. "We have a long way to go and we'd better start early in the morning."
No one knew it, but someone, or something, watched them while they slept.

Mrs. Beakley woke up when she felt something brush across her feet. She looked around, frightened. "Where am I?" she wondered.

She found herself in a rickety bed in the branches of a tree. Two monkeys were tickling her feet.

"How did I get here?" she asked herself. Holding onto a creeping vine, she slipped to the ground and went to find the others.

As she walked through the jungle, she met a lion.
"Help!" screamed Mrs. Beakley.
The lion was about to jump on her when a huge duck swung down on a vine, landing right between the old lady and the lion.
The duck fought off the lion and sent him running back into the jungle. Then the duck beat his chest and roared.
"Amazing!" said Mrs. Beakley.

The duck picked up Mrs. Beakley and carried her back to the tree house, swinging from vine to vine. There he handed her a piece of fruit.

"I don't understand," said Mrs. Beakley, frightened.

"Mizbeakey cook food for me," said the duck.

"You can talk!" she said. "And you know my name! But how?"

He showed her the tattoo on the bottom of his right foot.

"It's the Greydrake coat of arms!" she gasped. "I don't believe it! You're Prince Greydrake!"

And the duck replied, "Mizbeakey make food!"

Meanwhile, Launchpad, Scrooge and his nephews were searching for Mrs. Beakley, afraid for her safety.

"Maybe an elephant has eaten her!" said Dewey.

"Elephants are plant eaters," said Huey. "She was probably attacked by a lion."

"Stop it, you two!" said Scrooge. "We've got to find her before...*ulp*!"

Suddenly, they were surrounded by fierce men carrying spears.

Scrooge and the others were taken to a village of straw-and-mud huts. In the center of the village square was a wooden tower leading up to a platform, directly above a pool of steaming liquid.

"Boiling oil!" said Scrooge.

"I don't think they want us to find the Silver Bird," said Launchpad.

One of the warriors told Launchpad to climb the tower.

Launchpad climbed the steps nervously, the warrior pushing him from behind.

"Nice view," said the pilot, "but I've seen enough."

"Jump!" ordered the warrior.

"Are you crazy?" cried Launchpad.

"Jump!"

The warrior pushed him off the platform. But just before Launchpad fell into the boiling oil, Greydrake swooped down and caught him.

While the warriors were confused, Scrooge and his nephews grabbed vines and followed Greydrake to his hut. Mrs. Beakley was glad to see them. "Thank you for finding them, Greydrake," she said.

"Greydrake strong. Greydrake save," boasted the duck.

"Will someone tell me what's going on?" asked Scrooge. Mrs. Beakley told them the whole story.

"Isn't it wonderful?" she finished. "And I think he knows where the Silver Bird is."

"Then what are we waiting for?" cried Scrooge.

Greydrake led them to the site of an old plane crash.

Scrooge frowned. "So this is the legendary Silver Bird," he said. "I've come all this way for a pile of junk."

"Oh, it's not so bad, Mr. McD," said Launchpad. "It's a plane. It will fly us home."

Greydrake called up a herd of elephants. In no time, they had turned the plane right side-up.

"We'll need some fuel," said Scrooge.

"We'll go get some oil from that village," said Huey.

While Launchpad worked on the plane, Mrs. Beakley boiled the oil to make gasoline.

By nightfall, the plane was ready.
"We'll go first thing in the morning," said Scrooge.
"What about Greydrake?" asked Mrs. Beakley.
"We have to leave him here."

"No, we must take him home," said Mrs. Beakley. "He is King Greydrake now."

Suddenly, spears and arrows were flying all around them.

"The warriors have found us!" shouted Scrooge. "To the plane! Hurry!"

The Jungle Duck was with them when the plane took off.

The next day, they landed in the capital of Duckoslakia and learned that Greydrake's evil uncle, Goosepimple, was about to have himself crowned King. Scrooge and the others got there just in time to stop the ceremony.

"Wait!" cried Scrooge. "Here is the real King!"

The Jungle Duck held his uncle up in the air.

"Look!" cried one of the ministers, pointing to Greydrake. "He has the Greydrake crest on the sole of his foot."

The coronation took place, but with the real King. Mrs. Beakley looked on proudly.

"You have a big job ahead of you, Greydrake. I'm sure you will rule fairly."

"Yes, Mizbeakey," he answered. "I teach people things you teach me."